And there's more…

The Polish countess, Felicia Gizycka Magruder, ran off to San Diego and, happily trading her title for a waitress's tray, went to work in a coffee shop.

Stuey Ungar, a tenth-grade dropout, won the World Series of Poker at the age of 23. Ungar was New York's greatest card player ever, with a killer instinct and a disregard for money that made him unbeatable. Unfortunately, he also had a lifelong taste for fast living that forced his last hand in March 1999, at 42.

As typewriter repairman to the stars, Stanley Adelman fixed the cranky carriage returns of such luminaries as Isaac Bashevis Singer, Erich Maria Remarque, and David Mamet.

JANE O'BOYLE is a writer who lives in Charleston, South Carolina. Her other books include the first *Wrong!*, *Wrong Again!*, and *Free Drinks for Ladies with Nuts* (all available from Plume), and *Catnip for the Soul*.

Cool Dead People

Obituaries
of Real Folks
We Wish We'd Met
a Little Sooner

Jane O'Boyle

A PLUME BOOK

PLUME
Published by the Penguin Group
Penguin Putnam Inc., 375 Hudson Street, New York, New York 10014, U.S.A.
Penguin Books Ltd, 27 Wrights Lane, London W8 5TZ, England
Penguin Books Australia Ltd, Ringwood, Victoria, Australia
Penguin Books Canada Ltd, 10 Alcorn Avenue,
Toronto, Ontario, Canada M4V 3B2
Penguin Books (N.Z.) Ltd, 182–190 Wairau Road, Auckland 10, New Zealand

Penguin Books Ltd, Registered Offices:
Harmondsworth, Middlesex, England

First published by Plume, a member of Penguin Putnam Inc.

First Printing, April 2001

1 3 5 7 9 10 8 6 4 2

℗ REGISTERED TRADEMARK—MARCA REGISTRADA

LIBRARY OF CONGRESS CATALOGING-IN-PUBLICATION DATA

O'Boyle, Jane.
Cool dead people : obituaries of real folks we wish
we'd met a little sooner / Jane O'Boyle.
p.   cm.
ISBN 0-452-28229-2
1. Obituaries—United States. 2. Biography—20th century.
3. United States—Biography.
I. Title.
CT220 .O26 2001
920'.009'04—dc21   00-065283

Printed in the United States of America
Set in Century Expanded
Designed by Eve L. Kirch

For the coolest dead people I know

Lt. Col. James P. Atwood
Gilson "Jack" Bradish
Mark Suino
and
James E. O'Boyle

CONTENTS

Few are wholly dead:
Blow on a dead man's embers
And a live flame will start.

—Robert Graves

Cool Dead People

INTRODUCTION

More than two million people die each year in this country. As the greatest generation of the twentieth century dwindles down to a precious few, we seem ever more aware of the newspaper obituaries. They are strangely fascinating, if only because they say so much, so late—an entire life in only a few sentences. Yet obits speak volumes. Concisely crystallizing the meaning of a life, these words are dewdrops that form a small pool of uncontainable human spirit. Obituaries make us pause, and sometimes we even wonder: What will they write about me?

Many obituaries are of great statesmen and celebrities. Their lives garner a lot of space in the newspapers— well, if it's a slow news day, that is. If someone dies in the middle of a presidential impeachment or a great war, even a famous person will have her life severely edited in the obituary column. And when push comes to shove in the managing editor's office, there are those whose obituaries won't run at all. They aren't record holders, senators, or movie stars. But they are problem solvers, creators, advocates, trailblazers, curators, and dreamers. They are everyday people like you and me who did extraordinary things. And that makes them cool.

This is a collection of obituaries of some people you've probably never heard of. But now you will meet them and perhaps get a truer sense of the stuff from which our lives are made. These people may be dead, but they remind us that the world is filled with others just like them who are more interesting than we probably realize. The next time you meet an elderly lady or gentleman—or anyone, for that matter—look in their eyes for the cool person who is still very much alive.

Trailblazers

Thoroughly Modern Mariner

Frieda Mae Hardin died August 9, 2000, in Livermore, California. She was 103, the nation's oldest female veteran of the armed forces.

In 1918, before women could vote, Frieda Mae Green was working at a five-and-dime in Portsmouth, Ohio, when she decided to join the Navy. The Navy was recruiting women in order to free sailors for combat duty in World War I. Her mother was horrified when she enlisted and became a Yeoman F, or "yeomanette," as the women were known. She was assigned to the Norfolk Navy Yard in Virginia, where she served as a clerk. Other yeomanettes served as translators, camouflage designers, and recruiters.

Hardin never drank, smoked, or cursed, and there were no such things as tailhooks. She was released from duty in 1920. Women were not recruited into the Navy again until World War II, when they were called the Waves (Women Accepted for Volunteer Emergency Service). She survived four husbands, the last of whom was Robert Hardin. She wore her World War I naval uniform at a 1987 dedication in Arlington National Cemetery of the Women in Military Service for America Memorial. The monument honors the two million women who have served in this country's military.

"To those women now in military service, I say, 'Carry on,'" Hardin stated at the ceremony. "To those young women who may be thinking about a career in the military service, I say, 'Go for it!'"

Heaven Holds a Place
for Mr. Robinson

Mack Robinson, 85, died Sunday, March 12, 2000, in Pasadena, California. Robinson was a superb athlete, though his talents were overshadowed next to his younger brother, Jackie, the Baseball Hall of Famer. But Mack won a silver medal in the 1936 Olympic Games in Berlin, having come in second in the 200 meter race to gold medal winner Jesse Owens.

Mack almost hadn't made it to the Olympics. The trials were in New York and the Robinsons lived in Pasadena. A local businessman sponsored him, and he made the cut. He was sent to Berlin, where he ran second to Owens in the 200 meters, finishing at 21.1 seconds to Owens' 20.7.

"It's not too bad to be second best in the world at what you're doing, no matter what it is," recalled Robinson. "That makes you better than an awful lot of people."

Back home in 1937, Robinson set a national junior college record in the long jump of 25 feet 5½ inches, a record later broken by his brother Jackie. He won several national track titles while at the University of Oregon in 1938. Mack left college before graduation to become a street sweeper in Pasadena. But when a judge ordered all public pools to be opened to blacks, the town retaliated by firing all black city workers, including Robinson. He then worked in a variety of jobs, and retained a strong bond with his brother Jackie, who broke baseball's color barrier when he joined the Brooklyn Dodgers in 1947.

Mack Robinson participated in the Olympics again in 1984, when he joined several others in carrying the giant Olympic flag into the L.A. Memorial Coliseum.

The Stars Her Destination

Judy-Lynn Benjamin del Rey, 43, died from a brain hemorrhage in New York City on February 20, 1986. Although only four feet tall, del Rey was a giant among New York City book publishers, creating a market for science fiction and fantasy where there was none before. She discovered and published best-selling novelists Terry Brooks, Stephen Donaldson, David Eddings, William Goldman, and Piers Anthony, among dozens of others.

When presented with movie sketches for a story called "Star Wars," del Rey agreed to publish the unknown George Lucas's novel, three months before the movie's release made him a household name. Del Rey was a colorful figure who frequently wore sweeping capes to work and had an office in the Random House building guarded by the head of Chewbacca, Han Solo's Sasquatch-like partner.

She was given her own imprint within the company in 1977. Her first release at Del Rey Books was *The Sword of Shannara* by Illinois attorney Terry Brooks. When the novel went on the *New York Times* best-seller list, it was the first time any work of fiction had appeared on what was then the "trade paperback bestseller list." Not long after, the *Times* divided its best-seller list format into fiction and nonfiction categories. When she published William Goldman's novel, *The Princess Bride*, del Rey included an address within the story for those who wanted to read the missing romance scene. (Readers were to address requests to "Urban del Rey," which was the name of one of her pet ceramic bulls, a collection del Rey lovingly referred to as her "papal bulls.") The novel went on to become a landmark classic along with other Del Rey books, such as *The Mists of Avalon* by Marion Zimmer Bradley and the works of Isaac Asimov and Arthur C. Clarke. She is survived by her husband, the science fiction writer Lester del Rey.

Great Things
from Small Cars

Myron Scott, 91, died October 4, 1998, in Kettering, Ohio. As a newspaper photographer for the *Dayton Daily News* in 1933, Scott once happened upon six local boys racing wooden contraptions down Big Hill Road in Oakwood. He took their photograph, but it also gave him an idea. Scott asked the boys to gather some friends and have a race. With that, Scott started what he dubbed the All-American Soap Box Derby when he launched it a year later with 330 participants and more than 40,000 spectators.

Scott left the newspaper in 1939 and went to work in the advertising department at Chevrolet, which had sponsored the Soap Box Derby. In 1952, he was asked to come up with a name for a new European-style sports car, preferably a name that began with a C. Suggestions swirled around among department heads—Champion,

Celestial, Challenger. Scott flipped through a dictionary, and after he found the name of a small British warship, sent a note to Chevrolet's chief engineer, Edward Cole, which read: "How would you like to go for a ride today in my Corvette?" Chevrolet executives loved it.

Scott became the public-relations czar for the new Corvette, although he liked to remind people that he never got a bonus, a day off, or even a Corvette of his own as a reward. It remains Chevrolet's most successful vehicle. Today's soap box cars are sleek and plastic, built from kits, but the Derby still uses the logo designed by Scott many years ago.

Society Wife
Chose Frontier Life

Katherine Woodruff Fanning, the first woman to head the American Society of Newspaper Editors, died on October 20, 2000, in Boston. She was 73.

Born in Joliet, Illinois, Fanning was graduated from Smith College in 1949 and married Marshall Field IV in 1950. Field was editor and publisher of the *Chicago Sun-Times* and the *Chicago Daily News*, as well as chairman of the company that owned the Marshall Field chain of department stores. Fanning had three children and became known as "the Grace Kelly of Chicago." But she disliked the life of a society matron and felt a lack of independence or accomplishment. Fanning divorced Field and packed the three children into a station wagon and moved to Alaska.

She took a $2-an-hour job as a librarian at the struggling *Anchorage Daily News* and moved up the ranks as a reporter. In 1966, she married former *Sun-Times* editor Larry Fanning, and together, they bought the Anchorage newspaper. When her husband died in 1971, Katherine Fanning became editor and publisher. The paper soon received national recognition for news reporting, and she helped increase daily circulation from 12,000 to 50,000, making it the state's largest newspaper. Fanning directed the paper into delicate issues, such as critically examining the Trans-Alaskan pipeline, the role of guns in Alaskan society, and the land rights of local natives. In 1976, she edited a fifteen-part investigative series about the Teamsters union in Alaska, for which the paper was awarded the Pulitzer Prize.

Fanning left Alaska in 1983 to become editor of the *Christian Science Monitor*, the prestigious Boston-based national paper, where she also improved the content and increased circulation. In 1988, Fanning and two of her top editors resigned from the *Monitor* to protest cost-cutting and layoffs mandated by the paper's owner, the Christian Science church. She then became a fellow at Harvard University and Boston University, and served on the board of the Associated Press and the *Boston Globe* newspaper.

Windy City Sign-off

Clint Youle died in Galena, Illinois, on July 23, 1999, at the age of 83. Youle was credited as television's first weatherman, on the Chicago NBC affiliate during the 1940s and 1950s. He became a meteorologist during his years in the Army Air Force, and spent his early years writing about the weather for newspapers and radio. When TV station WNBQ took to the air in 1949, Youle volunteered to report the weather.

Left to his own creative devices, Youle ad-libbed his forecast and told folksy stories about local events while explaining the weather to viewers. He soon hit upon the idea of using a map as a visual aid. Youle went out and purchased a large Rand McNally map, covered it with Plexiglas and drew on it with a black marker so viewers could better understand his comments.

He had his own show, *The Weatherman*, at 10:00 P.M.,

and it was a great success. The first ever TV news ratings in Chicago ranked his program number one. During this era, Chicago became acclaimed for its innovative television programming. Using shoestring budgets and obscure personalities, local TV stations created a large number of successful programs. WNBQ (later to become WMAQ-TV) was one of the most original stations, and many of its programs were broadcast across the country. Unknown newsmen who worked with Youle at the time were Hugh Downs, Dave Garroway, and Studs Terkel.

On April 15, 1956, WMAQ was the first station in the country to broadcast entirely in color. Youle took full advantage of this by buying red and orange markers to add visual effects to his weather map. By 1960, the time slot for weather shows was decreasing, and Youle retired. He then ran several rural newspapers, and even patented a cattle guard device. Youle didn't live long enough to make it onto Willard Scott's *Today* show birthday tributes, but Scott wouldn't have made it without this pioneer TV weatherman.

The White Hat of Washington

C arl Maxey, 73, died on Thursday, July 17, 1997, in Spokane, Washington, the town from which he almost single-handedly desegregated much of the Pacific Northwest in the 1950s. He was eastern Washington's first black lawyer and used the courts to break down barriers at dozens of restaurants and private clubs. He also represented a number of clients, white and black, in several celebrated criminal cases.

Born out of wedlock in Tacoma, Maxey was adopted by a Spokane couple when he was 2 years old. However, he ended up spending most of his youth at the Spokane Children's Home, from which he was expelled at age 11 when the board unanimously voted to stop harboring "colored children" in 1936. He was eventually educated at an Indian school in Idaho, where a Jesuit priest sponsored him through high school and into the army as a medic in World War II. After the war, his boxing skills earned him scholarships to Oregon State University and Gonzaga University Law School, where he was light-weight boxing champion in 1950.

When Maxey was growing up in Spokane, "No Colored" signs were common around town, and blacks were only allowed in the Natatorium Park dance hall if a black band was playing. Blacks were not allowed in the park's pool at all.

"I've been thrown out of the Nat more times," Maxey once said, determined to change things when he became a lawyer in 1951. He built his career on the cases no one else wanted: divorces, larcenies, and anti-war activists. He was famous for his white suits and civil rights actions. He claimed many victories just by *threatening* to sue in this town where approximately 2 percent of the population is black. Maxey became a longtime civic leader and role model for underprivileged youth in Spokane. Judge John Schultheis recalled a conversation in which he told Maxey he was going to "throw the book" at his client.

"What am I supposed to tell my client?" Maxey replied.

"Tell him the judge is a stupid S.O.B.," Schultheis said.

"I already told him that," Maxey responded.

Maxey took his own life with a shotgun and left no note. Whatever the reason, said son Bill, "he kept it to himself." He is survived by his wife, Merrie Lou, and two sons who are lawyers in his firm.

The Soldier Chemist

Joshua Myron, a New York City pharmacist, died on June 8, 2000, at age 102. A dedicated Zionist, Myron began campaigning for a Jewish homeland back during World War I.

Along with Russian journalist Vladimir Jabotinsky, Myron helped recruit Jews from all over Europe and the Middle East, forming a Jewish brigade to fight alongside the British Army during the Great War. This brigade is often referred to as the Jewish Legion.

Myron was a company sergeant in this camel-mounted brigade, which fought against Turkey in Palestine. Many believe it was vital to the victory of the British war effort and therefore to the British announcing their support of a Jewish homeland in Palestine in 1917.

Myron was born in 1897 in Rishon Lezion, the first officially Zionist settlement in Palestine. This settlement had been financed by Edmond de Rothschild, who had a large vineyard there. Myron moved to the United States after World War II and obtained a pharmacy degree from Albany University. He devoted his life to the foundation of Israel, even after he moved to New York, where he owned two midtown pharmacies.

A Rose by the
Name of Blumkin

Rose Blumkin died in Omaha at age 104 in August 1998. A Russian immigrant who spoke no English, Mrs. Blumkin founded the Nebraska Furniture Mart in 1937 with $500 and built it into one of the nation's largest furniture stores. Her aggressive marketing included underselling her competitors, and she became a model for investor Warren Buffett, who bought majority control of the Mart in 1983.

"I didn't like to stay home," said Mrs. B. (as she was known), who was only four feet ten inches tall. "I was too lonely. I love work. It keeps you young. Lazy people don't last."

Mrs. Blumkin was born in Minsk, one of eight children. Her father, a rabbi, and her mother ran a grocery store, at which Mrs. Blumkin started working at age 6. When she was 20, she married Isadore Blumkin, a shoe salesman, and the couple moved to Omaha in 1919. They ran a secondhand clothing store and had four children. Mrs. Blumkin helped him out until she started her own business in 1937.

At one point, she sold everything in her own home to pay a debt. After her husband died in 1950, Blumkin's son Louis became her partner. Blumkin stayed active at Furniture Mart, running the carpeting division until 1989, when she had a dispute with her two grandsons, who were also top executives. Blumkin felt she was being left out of family business decisions. She soon started a rival business, Mrs. B's Carpets, right across the street from the Furniture Mart. The family repaired their rift. Buffet eventually bought the carpet business as well, in 1992.

Death of a Salesman

E dward Davis, the first black owner of a new car dealership in the United States, died in Detroit on May 3, 1999, at age 88. Davis worked at a Dodge plant in Detroit in the 1930s and opened a used-car lot in 1937. In 1940, by opening a Studebaker dealership, he became the first black man to open a new car showroom. When Studebaker went out of business in 1956, Davis decided to open a Chrysler showroom.

"It was tough," said Davis. "Banks wouldn't loan you any money, and sometimes it was hard to get people to work for you." He started out as a salesman at a local Chrysler-Plymouth dealership. He wasn't allowed to sell on the showroom floor with the white sales staff, so he converted a second-floor supply room into his office. He became a huge success, selling his products to the black community, and sold far more cars than any of the white salesmen. Finally, in 1963, he had earned enough money to buy his own Chrysler dealership. Davis Motors in Highland Park was the first black-owned "Big Three" car dealership in the country. Mr. Davis retired in 1971.

Curators

Candid Camera
Comrade

Lucienne Bloch died on March 13, 1999, at her home in Gualala, California. She was 90. The Geneva-born daughter of the noted Swiss composer Ernst Bloch, she was a glass sculptress and the focus of an acclaimed one-woman show in New York in 1931. While in New York, Bloch attended a banquet honoring the great muralist, Diego Rivera, who was in town for his exhibit at the Museum of Modern Art. The 22-year-old Bloch found herself seated next to the great muralist and they began an animated conversation in their common language, French. When a dark-haired woman came up behind Bloch and hissed "I hate you," Bloch burst out laughing. It was Frida Kahlo, Rivera's jealous wife. The three became good friends. Bloch never had an affair with Rivera, but she did become his unpaid assistant.

Soon after, Nelson A. Rockefeller commissioned Rivera to paint a 1,000-square-foot fresco in the great hall of the new Rockefeller Center, now known as the GE Building. During the Depression, with its competing currents of social change, the fiery Communist artist saw an opportunity to iconize Lenin on the newest American monument to capitalism. When it became apparent that Rivera was highlighting a portrait of Lenin as a charismatic leader, Rockefeller asked him to substitute an anonymous figure instead. Rivera refused. Rockefeller stationed guards around the work and made plans for its destruction.

In order to capture the mural before it was erased, Bloch walked into the RCA Building with a camera under her blouse. She snuck up onto a scaffold and took surreptitious photographs of the doomed mural. The photos are the only surviving record of Rivera's controversial work.

While working with Rivera, Bloch fell in love with his chief plasterer, a young Bulgarian named Stephen Dimitroff. They married and became an artistic team, painting frescoes all over the country, including her most acclaimed work, *The Evolution of Music*, at George Washington High School in upper Manhattan. They lived for a time in Flint, Michigan, where he was a union organizer and she photographed strikes for *Life* magazine. They eventually moved to Mill Valley, California, where Dimitroff operated a frame shop until 1965. The couple retired to Gualala, where Dimitroff died in 1996.

Black Widow
of the Civil War

Daisy Anderson of Denver died on September 19, 1998, at 97. She was one of three known surviving Civil War widows.

Anderson was 21 when she married 79-year-old Robert Ball Anderson. He was a former slave who had escaped Kentucky to join the Union Army when he was 22. After the war, he joined the buffalo soldiers on the western frontier.

She was born Daisy Graham in Hardin County, Tennessee, the daughter of a sharecropper with eight children. They picked cotton until the family moved to Arkansas in 1917 to escape racial tensions. She met Anderson after church one Sunday and they embarked on a thirty-day courtship. His mother had been sold and sent away from their Kentucky plantation when he was six, and he never saw her again. In April 1865, he had run away and joined the Union Army's 125th Colored Infantry.

After the Andersons married in 1922, they settled on Anderson's 2,000-acre ranch in Hemingford, Nebraska.

"I wanted a home," explained the widow. "I didn't have anything. I didn't have but one dress. We had no chairs; we ate standing up at the table. We met thirty days before we got married, and I loved him until the day he died."

Her husband wrote a memoir called *From Slavery to Affluence*, and died eight years after they were married. His widow lost the farm during the Depression and worked as a day laborer. She eventually became a poet and lecturer and moved to Steamboat Springs to be near her sister. Mrs. Anderson's death leaves two known Civil War widows who survive: Alberta Martin, 91, of Elba, Alabama, who was married to a Confederate soldier, and Gertrude Grubb Janeway, 89, of Blaine, Tennessee, whose husband was a Union soldier.

The Bunnies' Bridesmaid

E mily W. Reed died on May 19, 2000, in Cockeys-
ville, Maryland, at the age of 89. Reed was the Alabama state librarian who enraged segregationists back
in 1959 when she refused to withdraw from circulation a
children's picture book about a white rabbit who mar-
ries a black rabbit.

It was a time when blacks were struggling to gain
access to public libraries and other institutions in the
American South. *The Rabbits' Wedding* by Garth Williams
was published by Harper & Brothers in 1958. The book
had "no political significance" according to its author. But
the *Montgomery Home News* attacked the book on the
ground that it promoted racial integration. When Reed
admitted she liked the book and refused to ban it, the Alabama legislature had a measure introduced that would

require its state librarian to be a native of the state and a graduate of either Auburn or University of Alabama. Reed had been born in Asheville, North Carolina, and graduated from Indiana University. She moved to Washington, D.C., before the measure was enacted.

The book was banned.

All the News
That's Fit to Shout

F rancis Taylor Slate, 80, died in Mount Vernon, Virginia, on May 27, 1998. Slate, a retired Army colonel, was also the official town crier of the city of Alexandria for more than twenty years. He would frequently appear around town in Colonial costume, ringing an eighteenth-century handbell and shouting, "O-yez, o-yez, welcome one and all." The phrase "Hear ye" did not become common crier usage until after the 1770s.

Slate was Alexandria's first town crier in 200 years, when he began to appear in his burgundy frock coat and black three-cornered hat, in 1976. The unpaid position mostly consisted of leading parades and presenting honorary proclamations. In 1990, when he won an international competition of town criers, Slate's shouting was measured at 97 decibels.

Slate and his wife, Anne (who died in 1996), were history buffs. The colonel was born in New York, and in 1942, he became a second lieutenant and platoon leader with the 28th Infantry Regiment, also known as the Black Lions. He was promoted to captain on the battlefield in Europe, where he earned the Bronze Star and the Purple Heart. He also served in the Korean War and the Vietnam War, and retired in 1972.

Released
on Good Behavior

S aul Kane, 65, died in the Lexington, Kentucky, federal prison on January 20, 2000. Kane was a bonvivant and "wiseguy," a bail bondsman who owned and operated the My Way lounge on Pacific Avenue in Atlantic City, New Jersey. He was serving time for drug trafficking. Kane was a close personal friend of Nicodermo "Little Nicky" Scarfo, Sr., who is also in a federal prison. He was suspected to be Scarfo's financial advisor, so federal investigators referred to Kane as the "Meyer Lansky of the Boardwalk." But Kane insisted he and Scarfo were merely friends.

Kane spent the last thirteen years of his life behind bars, serving a ninety-five-year prison term, and he refused all overtures to turn evidence on Scarfo and gain early release. Before his death, Kane had arranged for a paid death notice in the *Philadelphia Inquirer* and *At-*

lantic City Press proclaiming Scarfo as his "brother," which, investigators believe, confirmed to his friend that he had never betrayed him.

"He went to his grave a wiseguy," said one investigator.

"He loved the controversy this kind of thing would stir," said Camden County Sheriff Michael McLaughlin. "He loved being in the mob spotlight." Kane once wrote a letter to one of the newspapers after his conviction.

"I do in fact have heroes ... my mother and father, daughter, David Ben Gurion, Dr. Salk, and all people who stand up and do the right thing," he explained. Investigators said he was still a convicted extortionist and drug dealer, but one law enforcement official said, "In a funny kind of way, he had a sense of honor."

Bubelah Bibliophile

Dina Abramowicz, 90, died in New York City on April 3, 2000. She was born in Vilna, Lithuania, the great center of Yiddish culture now known as Vilnius. Vilna was fiercely loved by its Jewish inhabitants, who called it the "Jerusalem of Lithuania." Abramowicz was the daughter of teachers, and when she was a youngster the city switched allegiances from the czar's empire to Poland, then to Lithuania, Germany, and finally, Russia. She grew up speaking Russian, but when the Germans occupied the town during World War I and allowed Jews to start their own schools, her parents sent her to a Yiddish school.

Abramowicz studied Polish literature at university, then went to work at the children's library of Vilna. She also joined YIVO, the Yiddish Scientific Institute, which soon became a repository of thousands of manuscripts and books of local Jewish scholars. In World War II, the city's 56,000 Jews were herded into the Vilna ghetto. There Abramowicz helped set up a makeshift library, although she recalled asking another librarian who would want to borrow books in such terrible conditions.

"Since there is nothing one can do about this absurd situation, what's the use of talking and wondering?" was the reply Abramowicz recalled later. In its first year, the library circulated more than 100,000 books, mostly escapist fiction.

The ghetto was eventually liquidated in 1942, and Abramowicz lost her mother in Treblinka. She herself escaped from a camp and, after the war, reunited with her father in New York. She met another surviving YIVO member from Vilna and joined him in reconstituting the collection in a Chelsea warehouse. The books had been smuggled out of Eastern Europe by former slave laborers known as the "paper brigade."

Abramowicz, who was only five feet tall, was the head librarian at YIVO in New York City for more than a generation. Her mind was a mental card catalog of hundreds of rare books and historical materials, which she would hunt down for scholars and writers, such as Irving Howe and Leon Uris. She received daily inquiries from journalists and writers about the Yiddish language and the history of Eastern Europe and religion. She left no survivors, but a unique collection of books, which she had shepherded across continents and through great wars.

A Most Congenial Shot

Photographer A. Stanley Terrick, the *Look* magazine photographer who captured John F. Kennedy, Jr., as a toddler peering out from under his father's desk in the Oval Office, died on July 19, 1999, in Gaithersburg, Maryland. He was 77. His death followed by only three days the death of his famous subject, who went down in a plane off Martha's Vineyard.

In October 1963, Terrick and President Kennedy had had to wait for the First Lady, Jacqueline Kennedy, to leave town. The President wanted his children photographed in the White House, but the First Lady was adamant that their privacy be protected. Sadly, Terrick's endearing family photos in *Look* magazine hit newsstands the same week the President was assassinated in Dallas.

"Jackie later told Stanley how happy she was that the

President and Stanley hadn't listened to her," wrote biographer Kitty Kelley. "If they had, she would not have had the photographs. This is a refrain in memos and letters later between the two of them."

In the years after the President's assassination, Terrick was invited on several vacations with Mrs. Kennedy and her children. Her favorite Terrick photograph was an old one from the presidential campaign, where Kennedy is reaching over in the front seat of a convertible to brush the hair out of his wife's eyes.

Terrick was born in Baltimore and trained as a photographer in the Marine Corps, serving in the Pacific during World War II. He worked for the *Washington Post* and United Press International. He went to *Look* magazine in 1960 and covered the Kennedys until the magazine folded in the 1970s. He then did still photography on movie sets such as *All the President's Men* and *Reds*.

A Line in the Sand

Maria Reiche, 95, died in Lima, Peru, on June 8, 1998. This German-born mathematician was a legend in Peru, where she spent half a century studying and protecting huge ancient drawings in the Peruvian desert. She single-handedly preserved the Nazca Lines, a set of mysterious pre-Columbian animal figures and geometric shapes scratched into the Nazca desert floor about 250 miles south of Lima.

Reiche was always passionate about numbers, and she studied mathematics in Hamburg until she left Germany in 1932. She was teaching high school math and translating scientific papers in her new homeland, Peru, when she met a visiting American, Dr. Paul Kosok, who was studying ancient irrigation systems along the Peruvian coast. Kosok had seen the lines from the top of a mountain and asked Reiche if she could discern a mathematical or astronomical connection.

Some of the figures etched in the desert are more than a mile long and can only be discerned from an airplane. The dozens of figures include a hummingbird, a whale, a condor, a monkey, a man, a spider, and a trapezoid. Reiche believed they were created by Nazca Indian priests, who used them to follow the stars in the night sky and to plan seasonal celebrations. They date from between 900 and 200 B.C. Before it became a tourist attraction in the 1980s, Reiche guarded the Nazca Lines zealously, even chasing trespassers after she was confined to a wheelchair by Parkinson's disease.

Reiche became a Peruvian citizen in 1994 and persuaded UNESCO to declare the 200 square miles a world heritage site in 1995. She gave all her money to a foundation to preserve the lines and was considered a national hero in Peru.

Though constant exposure to the desert sun eventually caused Reiche to go blind, she said, "I can see every line, every drawing, in my mind."

A Wright to Play
the Blues

Early Wright, 84, the first black disc jockey on Mississippi radio, died in Memphis, Tennessee, on December 10, 1999. Wright was born in Jefferson, Mississippi, in 1915 and grew up to become a mechanic with his own car repair business. He also managed a gospel singing group called the Four Star Quartet, and he caught the ears of the white owner of the Clarksdale station, WROX, in 1947.

For more than fifty years, Wright played blues and gospel that reached most of the Mississippi delta. Wright was famous for not identifying the artists he played—such as Muddy Waters, B.B. King, Pinetop Perkins, and Robert Nighthawk—because he felt his listeners should already know who they were. He was also appreciated for extemporizing his own commercials for local businesses, ignoring the prepared copy: "At M & F Grocery and Market, the aisles are so big that two shopping carts can pass each other and never bump into each other. And everything in the store has a price on it. You don't have to worry about what it costs because the price is right there on it."

Guy Malvezzi of Connerly's Shoe Store in Clarksdale said, "You got your money's worth with Early."

Wright worked six days a week until shortly before he died of a heart attack. He lost one daughter, Patricia, to brain cancer in 1981, when she was 29. He lost another daughter, Barbara, 41, to lung cancer in 1997.

His Finest Work

Robert McG. Thomas, Jr., an obituary writer for the *New York Times*, died in Rehoboth Beach, Delaware, on January 6, 2000. He was 60. Thomas created a new way to present obituaries, with a fresh style that brought the deceased to life in what had been, traditionally, a field of dry death notices. Among his memorable portraits were these: mechanical engineer Russell Colley, whom he described as "the father of the space suit, the Calvin Klein of space"; painter and musician Anton Rosenberg, who "embodied the Greenwich Village hipster ideal of 1950s cool to such a laid-back degree and with such determined detachment that he never amounted to much of anything"; and Howard C. Fox, the Chicago clothier "and sometime big-band trumpeter who claimed credit for creating and naming the zoot suit with the reet pleat, the reave sleeve, the ripe stripe, the stuff cuff, and the drape shape that was the stage rage during the boogie-woogie rhyme time of the early 1940s."

Gregarious and tall, Thomas hailed from Shelbyville, Tennessee, and attended Yale University where, he said, he "flunked out because he decided to major in New York rather than anything academic." He joined the *Times* in 1959 and served as crime reporter and sports writer before moving to the obituaries in 1995.

Code Warrior

Dooley D. Shorty, 88, died on June 4, 2000, in Albuquerque, New Mexico. Shorty was a Navajo who helped train the Marines' "Code Talkers" during World War II. The 421 Navajo Code Talkers were instrumental in the American victory over Japan.

Navajo is a language with no written form and was chosen by the Marines to be least likely to be deciphered by the enemy. Use of the Navajo language, virtually incomprehensible to any listener, had been confined to the reservation for a long time. Although the amazingly adept Japanese cryptographers cracked almost every other Allied code, they never came close to interpreting these Marine communications.

Dooley Shorty was born on the Navajo reservation in Cornfields, Arizona. Shorty was one of 29 natives who helped devise new Navajo words for military terms by giving old words a second meaning. For example, *taschizzie* means "swallow" in Navajo, and Shorty designated this word for a torpedo plane. *Ja-sho*, "buzzard," meant bomber, and so forth.

This assignment was the first time Shorty had left the reservation or seen the ocean. In the first two days of the battle at Iwo Jima, Navajos sent or received 800 messages without error. After the war ended, the code was considered so valuable that it remained classified for twenty-three years. Shorty later taught silversmithing for thirty years at the Intermountain Indian School. Approximately 150 Code Talkers survive, each of whom recently received a Navajo G.I. Joe action figure, released by Hasbro in February 2000.

Diary of a Frank

Elfriede "Fritzi" Frank died in London at age 93 on October 1, 1998. She was born Elfriede Markovits in Vienna, and when Adolf Hitler annexed Austria in 1938, she fled to the Netherlands with her first husband, Erich Geiringer, and their two children, Heinz and Eva. The family settled into Amsterdam, where daughter Eva became friends with a young neighbor named Anne Frank. The Geiringer family received a summons to a German work camp and went into hiding, like the Frank family, in July 1942. They were betrayed nearly two years later and sent to Auschwitz, where Fritzi's husband and son perished.

She and her daughter were on a train in January 1945, returning to the Netherlands after the Russians had liberated their camp. Eva recognized another passenger on the train—Otto Frank, the father of her friend Anne. Eva introduced Frank to her mother, and they learned he was the sole survivor of the Frank family after Auschwitz.

"They helped each other come to terms with their losses," said the spokesperson for the Anne Frank Educational Trust UK. Frank consulted Fritzi about whether to publish his daughter's diary, which chronicled how her family hid in a secret annex. The diary was published in 1947 and became an immediate classic. Fritzi and Otto Frank were married in 1953 and settled in Switzerland, where they gave interviews and lectures about the atrocities of the Holocaust. Frank died in 1980.

Tuna Helper

rank Mather, a Woods Hole specialist on bluefin
tuna and the first to create a fish tagging system,
died in Falmouth, Massachusetts, on March 29, 1999, at
age 89.

Mather was an MIT-educated yacht designer who
helped design ships for the Navy during World War II.
Returning to Massachusetts, he became a research asso-
ciate at the Woods Hole Oceanographic Institute on Cape
Cod. He was also a dedicated angler who kept records
of every fish he ever caught. When he started noticing
changes in migratory patterns and growth rates, he
started marking his catch and releasing them. In the
early 1950s, Mather designed a tag attached to a streamer
that could be attached to fish. He found a sympathetic
audience in game fishermen up and down the coast, who
were happy to help tag fish. In 1959, five years after he

started tagging fish, two of his tuna from Long Island Sound were captured off the coast of France. Mather decided that the bluefin tuna was one long-lived stock that ranged from the Arctic Circle to the Cape of Good Hope, from the North Sea to the Gulf of Mexico. Tuna tagged in the Bahamas roamed up to 18 years, as far north as Norway and south to Argentina.

Mather's global system soon indicated near extinction of the tuna in the 1970s, which forced strict conservation measures. He became an honored member of fishing clubs from Hawaii to the Ivory Coast.

God's Witness

The Reverend Luigi Marinelli, 73, died on October 23, 2000, in Rome. He was a monsignor who worked at the Vatican for 45 years before his retirement in 1997. Marinelli provoked the ire of the Vatican when he anonymously published a best-selling exposé called *Via Col Vento in Vaticano*, or "Gone With the Wind in the Vatican." The book portrayed several loosely veiled church officials as corrupt, power-hungry, and sexually adventurous. One anecdote involved a prelate with a cash-filled suitcase being stopped at the Swiss border; another told the story of a bishop charged with sexually abusing a youngster.

Marinelli was summoned in 1999 to appear before a Roman Catholic court to answer questions about the book, but he declined, saying he could not recant.

"The book does not question the sanctity of Jesus

Christ, the Eucharist, or the Catholic Church," said the monsignor. "It just points out that the Vatican is made up of men, like me, who are flawed."

The Vatican then ordered the books removed from bookstores. This prompted the little-known book to become a national bestseller in Italy.

Marinelli's family held the funeral in a small church in his southern hometown, Cerignola, after they were asked not to hold the service in the local cathedral.

Creators

Wayne's World

Wayne McAllister, 92, died in Arcadia, California, on March 22, 2000. He was the West Coast architect who created the Sands and El Rancho hotels in Las Vegas, and the Brown Derby restaurant in Los Feliz, elevating flamboyant buildings into art forms. In the wake of the rapid development in the western states, many of them no longer exist.

Born in San Diego, McAllister dropped out of school to work for an architect in the 1920s. He was twenty when he designed the Agua Caliente resort in Mexico, which was frequented by Hollywood stars, such as Clark Gable, Jean Harlow and Gloria Swanson. He also refined the drive-in restaurant, turning it into a high-concept Los Angeles dining experience in the 1940s, with Simon's Drive-In and Bob's Big Boy, a low-slung mustard colored drive-in on Riverside Drive. Critic Alan Hess said that McAllister recognized that "the world was being shaped by the automobile." Bob's Big Boy is now considered an outstanding example of Art Moderne architecture. Many of McAllister's other buildings, however, were razed during the 1970s and 1980s, when critics did not appreciate his style.

In 1956, McAllister moved to Washington, D.C., where he gave up architecture to become vice president of the Marriott Corporation. He returned to Los Angeles in 1962 to develop coin-operated copying machines. Monuments to McAllister include several Los Angeles landmarks: Bob's Big Boy on Riverside is now a California State Point of Historical Interest.

God Rest His Sole

Roger Vivier, 90, died in Toulouse, France, on October 2, 1998. A shoe designer from the 1930s to the 1960s, Vivier created the squared toe and the stiletto heel, as well as original designs for many movie stars and royal families. He also created the "comma" heel, a curved steel design he worked on with aeronautical engineers, as well as the "choc," a high heel that curved dramatically inward toward the arch of the foot.

"People try to copy him," said shoe designer Manolo Blahnik, "but it's impossible to find that mix of technical skill and design."

Vivier was orphaned as a child and grew up with his aunt in Paris, where he studied sculpture. Designer Elsa Schiaparelli joined forces with Vivier, as did designers such as Christian Dior and Yves Saint Laurent. Vivier had a shop in Paris and another in New York City. His clients included Elizabeth Taylor, Marlene Dietrich, and Sophia Loren. When Queen Elizabeth II was crowned in 1953, she wore a pair of Vivier gold leather shoes that were encrusted with 3,000 garnets.

Nonconformist
Street Performist

Steven Slepack, a man who gave up a promising career in marine biology to become Professor Bendeasy, a Central Park street performer who wore a tuxedo and delighted children by twisting balloons into animal shapes, died on February 6, 1996, in Rochester, Vermont. He was 46.

Slepack was born and raised in Brooklyn, and won a full science scholarship to the University of Hawaii. Once arriving in the Aloha State, he fell in love with the beach and the banjo and soon dropped out of school, though he remained a voracious reader. He returned to New York and started playing the banjo on the streets, eventually moving on to balloon twisting. As Professor Bendeasy, he could blow up a long balloon in a single breath and turn the balloon into an exotic bird or a dog.

In the 1970s, he traveled through San Francisco,

where he taught balloon twisting to a young comedian named Steve Martin. He moved on to Paris, then returned to New York, to his familiar post near Central Park's Alice in Wonderland statue or the front door of F.A.O. Schwartz toy store.

He drove an old ambulance and often sold music tapes of his favorite 1920s jazz artists. In 1990, Slepack married a young woman named Catlin Hill, who changed her name to Princess Oulala, donned harlequin stockings, and joined his act. He is survived by the Princess, as well as his mother and grandmother.

Cradle to Grave,
Blues and a Shave

A rchie L. Edwards, 79, died in Seat Pleasant, Maryland, on June 18, 1998. Edwards was a barber on Bunker Hill Road in northeast Washington, D.C., for 39 years, but he was better known as an advocate for blues music. He founded the D.C. Blues Society in 1987, which held meetings and jam sessions in his two-chair barber shop. Edwards also loved African-American folk narratives, and wrote original songs such as "Saturday Night Hop" and "Baby, Please Gimme a Break."

Edwards was a regular performer at the Prince George's Community College blues festival and the Blue Ridge Folk Life Festival in Ferrum, Virginia. He toured Europe with the American Folk Blues Festival in the 1970s, and recorded two albums: *Blues 'N Bones* and *Living Country Blues, Volume Six: The Road Is Rough and*

Rocky. He was adamant that people understand the African roots of blues music.

"People today, they say they like blues music," Edwards once remarked, "but they don't know the first thing about it. It's going to hell, because there ain't enough people like me to correct 'em."

Edwards was born in Union Hall, Virginia, and learned to play guitar from his father, a sharecropper who frequently played music with friends. Edwards refined his musical skills while playing at private parties when he worked as a cook and chauffeur in New Jersey and Ohio. He settled in the D.C. area after serving as an Army military police officer during World War II. In addition to barbering, Edwards was a truck driver for the city of Washington and spent 30 years as a guard in the Federal Protective Service.

If Life Is a Bowl of Cherries, Bunny Made It Taste Sweeter

Aaron "Bunny" Lapin, 85, died July 10, 1999, in Los Angeles, at age 85. Lapin put whipped cream in a spray can more than fifty years ago and named it Reddi-wip, a postwar symbol of America's demand for convenience and a fine dessert topping. Mr. Lapin's product was originally distributed in St. Louis, but demand grew far and wide. Today, Reddi-wip still comprises half of all dessert topping consumed in the United States and Canada.

Lapin started out as a St. Louis clothier but moved into the food sales business with Sta-Whip, a wartime substitute for whipping cream. After the 1946 invention of the Spra-tainer, a seamless aerosol canister, Lapin became the first to find a way to use it. He even refined the valve and patented the modification for himself. He first used the cans for shaving cream, but he found it was more profitable to sell his valves to other more established shaving cream companies. So Lapin put his dairy experience to use to patent Reddi-wip instead and moved to Los Angeles in 1954 to take the product nationwide.

Lapin eventually sold Reddi-wip to Beatrice Foods Inc. In December 1998, Lapin was named by *Time* magazine as one of the business geniuses of the century. The magazine listed Reddi-wip as one of the century's 100 great things for consumers, alongside the pop-top can and Spam.

Lava Makes the World
Go Round

Edward Craven Walker, 82, died on August 15, 2000, in London. Best remembered as the inventor of the lava lamp, Walker was also a nudist who made several movies promoting life in the buff.

"If you buy my lamp, you won't need drugs," Walker said of his oil and water lamp design, which he launched in 1963 as the "Astro lamp."

Walker was born in Singapore, and served on reconnaissance missions for the Royal Air Force in World War II. After the war, he visited the Isle du Levant off France and became interested in the nudist lifestyle. He made films about nudists, including *Eves on Skis* (1958) and *Traveling Light* (1960), which enabled him to open his own nudist resort in Bournemouth, on the south coast of England. He caused a stir in the community, however, when he tried to ban overweight people from his resort.

"It's not what naturism should be about," he commented about the heavyset.

When his lamp regained popularity in the 1990s, Walker explained its appeal:

"It's like the cycle of life. It grows, breaks up, falls down, and then starts all over again."

He Wrote It in Stone

John Petrillo died on April 16, 1999, in Mount Vernon, New York, at age 86. The memorial service for the stone maker was held in his family church, under a limestone and marble altar he'd built himself.

Petrillo joined his father's stone business in Mount Vernon after he graduated from the University of North Carolina in 1935. His career was interrupted by World War II, in which he served in many European theaters, including at the Battle of the Bulge. He returned to run the stone business with his brother, August, who eventually became mayor of Mount Vernon.

The Petrillo Stone Corporation built the limestone towers of Rockefeller Center, Radio City Music Hall, Fordham University, Lincoln Center, as well as the Sacred Heart Cathedral in Newark, New Jersey, and the Shrine of the Immaculate Conception in Washington,

D.C. Petrillo created the first travertine façade in New York City, at Harry Winston on Fifth Avenue. Travertine is an unusual limestone more commonly found in the great buildings of Italy. But Petrillo's favorite creation was one of his earliest: the gothic stone tower that dominates the Fordham campus in the Bronx.

Problem
Solvers

He Gave a
Goose Golden Legs

W. E. Fleming died on December 31, 1999, in Grand Island, Nebraska, at the age of 77. He received acclaim after he adopted a goose in 1988: He had observed the goose struggling to walk and realized that the animal had stumps instead of feet, so it pushed itself along on its chest. Fleming named the goose Andy, and fitted the goose with size 0 baby tennis shoes. Using a leash, Fleming taught Andy to walk. Together they made an appearance on *The Tonight Show with Johnny Carson* in 1989, and in *People* magazine in 1991. Nike gave Andy a lifetime supply of little tennis shoes.

Tragically, Andy the goose was kidnapped on October 19, 1991, and later found murdered in a ballpark in nearby Hastings. Fleming, a retired manufacturer, received $10,000 in donations from fans who wanted to offer a reward for information about the crime. The bird had been found mutilated, with his wings and head missing, leading some to surmise the killers were part of a satanic cult. The goose's corpse was still wearing the little tennis shoes.

"We pursued the case pretty hard," said Adams County Sheriff Gregg Magee. "We received lots of leads we followed up on, but we never had enough evidence to prosecute." The killer has never been found.

Stand By

Irving Strobing, 77, died at a veterans' hospital in Durham, North Carolina, on July 8, 1997. Strobing was one of a few thousand American soldiers in the Philippines during the very worst days of the war against Japan in 1942. They had retreated down the Bataan peninsula to make a last stand against overwhelming Japanese forces at a Manila Bay island known as Fort Corregidor. It was six months after Pearl Harbor and two months since General MacArthur had fled the Philippines for Australia.

Corporal Strobing was a 22-year-old radio operator in the signal corps from Brooklyn, New York. In the hour before he and his colleagues were ordered to surrender, Strobing kept up a stream of telegraph transmissions that were read over the radio and reprinted in national newspapers three weeks later. He described the horrors of the troops' last resistance to assault and the destruction of their own supplies to keep them from the enemy.

"I feel sick at my stomach. I am really low down. They are around now smashing rifles. They bring in the wounded every minute. We will be waiting for you guys to help.

"We are waiting for God knows what," he tapped. "How about a chocolate soda?

"Damage terrific. Too much for guys to take. Enemy heavy cross-shelling and bombing. They have got us all around and from the skies.

"The jig is up. Everyone is bawling like a baby. They are piling dead and wounded in our tunnel. Arm's weak from pounding key, long hours, no rest, short rations, tired." Finally, not knowing if he would survive, Strobing sent a message to his family. "God bless you and keep you. Love. Sign my name and tell my mother how you heard from me. Stand by."

Then, no more. Three years later, Strobing was released from a Japanese prison camp and introduced to Sgt. Arnold Lappert, the man who had transcribed his messages in Hawaii. Strobing also learned that his messages had provided vital information to military command. Strobing left the Army in 1949 and worked for the Federal Aviation Authority and the Department of Agriculture. He retired to North Carolina in 1980, where he started an amateur radio club. He is survived by his sister.

Racist Turned Rat

G ary Thomas Rowe, Jr., 64, died on May 25, 1998, in Savannah, Georgia. Rowe was an FBI informer who helped infiltrate the Ku Klux Klan, helping to convict three Klansmen of killing civil rights volunteer Viola Liuzzo in Selma, Alabama, in 1965.

Rowe testified that night-riding Klansmen shot Liuzzo, a white homemaker from Detroit, as she was driving demonstrators into town. He helped convict the three men to ten years in prison, then swiftly disappeared into the federal witness protection program. He remained a controversial figure, as some accused him of improperly participating in the Klan violence he was reporting to the FBI. In 1975, Rowe appeared wearing a cotton hood before a Senate Select Committee on Intelligence, testifying that the FBI knew about his participation in violence against blacks. Although he was an admitted racist, he was a better informer. In later years, Liuzzo's children unsuccessfully sued the FBI for $2 million, claiming that they had poorly trained Rowe, who could perhaps have saved their mother.

Under the federal witness protection program, Rowe had settled in Savannah and assumed the name Thomas Neal Moore, the name with which he was buried.

Soul of an Old Machine

Stanley Adelman of Manhattan died of heart failure on November 30, 1995, in Takoma Park, Maryland, at the age of 72. His typewriter repair shop on the Upper West Side was an emergency room for the cranky carriage returns of such luminaries as Isaac Bashevis Singer, Erich Maria Remarque, Philip Roth, Howard Fast, and David Mamet.

Adelman was born in Poland and was fluent in English, Yiddish, Polish, German, and Russian, which helped him work on a variety of international keyboard designs for old typewriters. His customers cherished his talent for fixing their favorite machines. When Adelman suggested Howard Fast buy a 1949 Underwood typewriter, Fast told him that, as a Jew, he felt he could not type on a German typewriter.

"I was in a concentration camp," replied Adelman. "If

I can sell that typewriter, you can write on it." Fast bought the machine.

Adelman had planned a career as a marine engineer before spending World War II in five different concentration camps. When he was freed, he started repairing typewriters instead, because he had become intrigued by the world of literature. He learned English by reading Stephen Crane's novel *The Red Badge of Courage* (which had been written in longhand, not on a typewriter). He was hired at Karl Osner's repair shop in New York City in 1951 and bought the shop from Osner when he retired in 1968.

Viva Bazata

Douglas DeWitt Bazata, a soldier of fortune who served with the United States Office of Strategic Services (OSS) in Europe during World War II, died July 14, 1999, in Chevy Chase, Maryland, at the age of 88. Born in Wrightsville, Pennsylvania, Bazata studied at Syracuse University and joined the Marines, serving from 1933 to 1937. He went on to become an Army officer in 1942, when he joined the OSS, the forerunner of today's Central Intelligence Agency.

He joined an elite squad of Allied guerillas known as Operation Jedburgh, a daring group of parachutists who volunteered for a "highly hazardous" mission behind enemy lines in Nazi-occupied France. The "Jeds" were dropped in three-man international teams to aid resistance leaders against the German occupiers. In 1944, Bazata parachuted into the Haute Saone region with two others, with the team code Cedric. He located a British secret agent known as Emile, and together they assisted the Maquis, the French anti-Nazi guerillas. They succeeded in evading capture by the Germans, including one close call where Emile and Bazata had to pretend to be Frenchmen gathering wild mushrooms. Emile (real name George Millar) wrote after the war that "walking with the tempestuous Bazata toward the German lines was like riding a horse with a mouth of iron."

Bazata won the Purple Heart four times, as well as the Distinguished Service Cross and France's Croix de Guerre with two palms. After the war, he turned to wine making and oil painting. His works of abstract expressionism were featured in one-man shows around the world. In the 1970s, he moved to Maryland to operate a pheasant preserve and hunting club. He also worked for the Veterans Administration and was special assistant to Secretary of the Navy John F. Lehman, Jr., during the Reagan administration.

Doctor Heals Town
Before Her Death

Dr. Peggy Rummel died in Colquitt County, Georgia, on May 7, 1999. She was 43 and suffered from liver cancer.

Born in South Carolina, Dr. Rummel moved to the remote Georgia county of 6,400 residents in 1983. She wanted to practice rural medicine and found the perfect home in this one-stoplight town. She raised eight foster children and became a prominent community member by helping to organize the high school prom and Easter egg hunts, in addition to running the county's 38-bed hospital.

"We need to be proud of the little places," she said, "and not assume that because it's small, it's inadequate."

When Dr. Rummel was diagnosed with cancer in January and given only eight weeks to live, she started making phone calls to find someone who would take over her practice. She also posted a letter on the Internet.

Eventually Dr. Rummel hired her replacement, Dr. Ifekan-Shango Simon. Within a day or two, Dr. Rummel started bleeding internally, but she still objected to the timing. She didn't want to die while her son, Richard, a premed student at Georgia Southwestern University, was taking his finals. So she decided to have blood transfusions until he could make it back to be with her. When he did, only then was she ready to go. Dr. Rummel was cremated, and according to her wishes, her ashes were scattered over Colquitt. A patient room at Miller County Hospital will be renovated and dedicated to her.

The Grapes of Reason

L ionel Steinberg, a table grape grower who became the first grower to sign a contract with Cesar Chavez and the United Farm Workers, died March 7, 1999, in Palm Springs, California. He was 79.

Steinberg was a major grower in the Coachella Valley and the longtime president of David Freedman & Co., a 1,200-acre vineyard in Thermal, which had been founded by his stepfather. Steinberg pioneered ways to grow new grape varieties by using special methods of pruning and harvesting. In the late 1960s, he stood alone among growers in his willingness to negotiate with Chavez and his union. He signed the historic contract with Chavez on April 10, 1970.

"He believed in a better life for farm workers," said his son, Billy, a Los Angeles songwriter.

"He was most comfortable, really, with people of the

soil," said his wife, Katrina. The couple often inspected farms and vineyards in their travels around the world. Steinberg's pact with Chavez (who died in 1993) sent shock waves through the agricultural world. Within months, most of the other grape growers in the state followed suit. Steinberg's leadership helped end a five-year strike and a devastating consumer boycott of grapes.

A graduate of Fresno State University, Steinberg was also a philanthropist, board member of Ben-Gurion University of the Negev as well as the University of California, and past chairman of the California Board of Agriculture. Most of his vineyards were sold in the 1980s and 1990s.

Hitler's Fräulein Friday

Gerda Christian, a personal secretary to Hitler who stayed with the Nazi dictator until his final days in a Berlin bunker, died in a Dusseldorf hospital in 1997. She was 83. Her death was reported by the newspaper *Bild* on Tuesday, July 15, but it is not clear when she died. She had entered the hospital in May.

Mrs. Christian rarely spoke about her work with Hitler. "What am I supposed to say about that?" she once asked. "Whatever I say would certainly be misinterpreted."

Mrs. Christian and Hitler's other private secretary, Gertrude Junge, remained with the Nazi ruler during his final days. They were among the inner circle of associates who attended his bunker wedding on April 28, 1945, to his longtime mistress Eva Braun. Hitler and Braun committed suicide two days later, and Mrs. Christian was one of those to whom he bid his last farewells. Mrs. Christian was sought as a witness at the Nuremberg tribunal, but she went into hiding after being released from an internment camp near Frankfurt. She never testified.

While in Hitler's service she met and married his Luftwaffe liaison officer, Gen. Eckhard Christian. According to the newspaper, Mrs. Christian once told close friends that Hitler was a fine boss and she had no complaints about her time working with the Nazi leader.

Lawyer Helped Sioux

Marvin J. Sonosky, a Washington, D.C., lawyer who championed the cause of the American Indian throughout his long career, died on July 16, 1997, in Alexandria, Virginia. He was 88. He was still an active senior partner in Sonosky, Chambers, Sachse & Endreson, the firm he formed in 1976 in Washington, D.C., with affiliate offices in Anchorage and Juneau, Alaska.

Mr. Sonosky specialized in the law relating to American Indians and served as general counsel to Assiniboine, Sioux, and Shoshone tribes in Montana, Wyoming, and the Dakotas. He successfully litigated many of their land claims against the federal government. In the most famous instance, he worked for 24 years—without pay—to get the United States to return the Black Hills of South Dakota to the Sioux nation. Considered sacred grounds by the Sioux, the hills had been taken from them in 1876.

In 1980, 104 years later, the United States Supreme Court finally ruled in the Indians' favor. It was the largest judgment ever entered against the United States on an Indian claim. Mr. Sonosky and two colleagues later shared an astonishing $10 million legal fee awarded them by the Federal Court of Claims in Washington, D.C., which was paid by the U.S. government.

Mr. Sonosky subsequently helped draft legislation to protect Indian rights and used his landmark fee to endow the Martin J. Sonosky Chair at his alma mater, the University of Minnesota Law School.

Hail to the Chief

L eRoy Gorham died at age 78 on July 3, 2000, in Chapel Oaks, Maryland. Gorham was born and raised in Bottom, Maryland, and served in the Army during World War II. In the summer of 1946, a house fire took the lives of Gorham's three children, Ruth, 4, Jean, 3, and LeRoy Earl, 2.

"The whole sky was lit up," recalled Gorham's best friend, Roy Lee Jordan. Firefighters took an exceptionally long time to arrive on the scene, in a predominantly African-American neighborhood that had no indoor toilets or running water. Residents tried to help with buckets of water, to no avail. When firefighters from the District of Columbia finally arrived, there were no hydrants to hook their hoses up to. Jordan recalled the anguish on Gorham's face when he learned about the fate of his children.

"His heart just broke," said Jordan. "It broke all our hearts."

Mobilized by his grief, Gorham took action. Within a year, he and a group of friends founded the Chapel Oaks Volunteer Fire Department, the first all-black volunteer fire company in Maryland, as it remains today. The men encountered resistance from white firefighters and received no financial assistance from any public source. They raised money from local residents to operate a small used pumper out of a dilapidated garage. The volunteer crew didn't have helmets, coats, or boots but were always the first to respond when a call went out from the surrounding black neighborhoods, as well as white neighborhoods. Eventually, the men constructed a brick firehouse, and in 1960, they were allowed to join the local fire association. Gorham served as its chief for 17 years, supervising hundreds of volunteer calls that saved countless families.

Gorham and his wife, Lillian, went on to have three more children. After Lillian died in 1991, he continued making his daily visits at the Chapel Oaks fire station. Gorham died of a heart attack and was buried in his dress-blue fire department uniform in Harmony, not too far from the great granite obelisk on Sheriff Road that memorializes his lifelong endeavors to save children and families.

Advocates

Final Round
Takes Braverman

Al Braverman, a "mashed face" former boxer, fight manager, and trainer, died on Saturday, July 5, 1997. He was 78. The cause was complications from diabetes. Mr. Braverman, unbeaten as a heavyweight from 1938 to 1941, managed more than thirty boxers in the 1940s and 1950s. He became well known for his injured face and Runyonesque style of speaking. Five of his fighters fought for world titles, including Chuck Wepner, known as the Bayonne Bleeder, who went nine rounds with Sonny Liston, incurring cuts that required 75 stitches. After the fight, Liston was asked if Wepner was the bravest opponent he had ever faced.

"No," Liston said, "but his manager is."

Wepner also fought Muhammed Ali for the world heavyweight championship in 1975. Before the fight, Mr. Braverman told reporters, quite seriously, that he had a salve that he put on the fighter's face to keep him from bleeding, and that no chemist had ever been able to completely break down the compound.

"But Al," someone asked, "won't they complain about using a foreign substance?"

"It ain't a foreign substance," Mr. Braverman replied, "It's made right here in the United States."

Ali won the fight in the 15th round. Mr. Braverman went to work for Don King in 1975 as director of boxing. Mr. Braverman later ran an antique store with his wife, Renée.

Jill of All Trades

Connie Clausen, an actress and literary agent who began her career by riding circus elephants, died of a stroke on September 7, 1997, at Lenox Hill Hospital in Manhattan. She was 74 and lived in Manhattan. Clausen's career began in the 1940s when she rode elephants for the Ringling Brothers and Barnum & Bailey Circus, a perfect training ground for work in the film business. She went to work at M-G-M studios in Hollywood, rising from messenger to director of special promotions. In New York, she landed several roles on Broadway and television, and wrote her memoir, *I Love You Honey, but the Season's Over*. She was a natural at promotion, and her book was a huge success. So she became a publicity agent for Macmillan Publishing in the 1970s. She helped launch two huge international best-sellers,

Watership Down and *Jonathan Livingston Seagull*, for the company.

She left Macmillan in 1976 to start her own agency, Connie Clausen & Associates, which was a pioneer in the so-called beauty book, beginning with a series of bestsellers by the photographer Francesco Scavullo. Other successful categories for Clausen were memoirs and biographies, including the Pulitzer Prize–winning *Jackson Pollock: An American Saga* by Steven Naifeh and Gregory Smith, and Quentin Crisp's *Resident Alien: The New York Diaries*.

Two Thumbs Up

William Stokoe, Jr., 80, died on April 4, 2000, in Chevy Chase, Maryland. Dr. Stokoe grew up on a farm in Stafford, New York, and after college went to teach English at Gallaudet University in Washington, D.C., in 1955. As with all professors at the only university devoted to the hearing-impaired, Stokoe was expected to teach without using sign language. Ever since an international symposium in 1880, there had been a movement away from sign language, and schools for the deaf preferred using lip-reading and attempts at oral communication. Proponents of this teaching method believed it would give deaf students their best chances in a hearing world.

Among themselves, however, Skokoe noticed that the students rattled away to each other in sign language.

"He underwent a sort of conversion, an epiphany and

a revelation," explained Stokoe's friend, Dr. Oliver Sacks. Stokoe realized that signing was a language in itself and deserved international recognition. He published ground-breaking books, *Sign Language Structure* and *A Dictionary of American Sign Language*, and founded the journal *Sign Language Studies*. He was generally acknowledged to be a stubborn man, scornful of linguists who believed lack of speech meant lack of language.

"Instead of seeing language in a different channel, the naïve observer, hearing no speech, supposed language was absent too," he wrote.

Gradually, his idea was accepted at Gallaudet and other schools for the deaf, and it is now common for those schools to use both signing and oral methods of instruction. He became highly respected by deaf students. Many students also credit Skokoe with encouraging Gallaudet to name its first deaf president in the 1980s.

Stokoe was an avid bagpipe player and belonged to the Washington Scottish Pipe Band. He enjoyed frequenting the Gallaudet campus in his kilt, rehearsing the bagpipes. The students frequently joked that those occasions made them grateful to be deaf, as Stokoe's pipe-playing was known sometimes to resemble monotonous screeching.

Bluebird Man
Beyond the Rainbow

A rt Aylesworth, an insurance agent and Montana conservationist, died of cancer on May 1, 1999. He was 72. Originally a dairy farmer, a back injury forced him into a second career in insurance. Aylesworth's pioneering work in goose nesting sites and other habitat restoration laid the groundwork for many conservation organizations. But he is best known among those organizations as "The Bluebird Man," for his particular passions, the endangered mountain and the western bluebirds. In 1974, Aylesworth took some scrap lumber and built a few nest boxes. He began giving the boxes away to anyone who would put them out and monitor their success. His project led to there being more than 35,000 bluebird nest boxes across the entire state.

In 1979, Aylesworth founded the Mountain Bluebird Trails group, which he headed until his death. When

Aylesworth discovered in 1982 that the hole in the nest boxes he'd distributed was fine for the western bluebird but one sixteenth of an inch too small for the mountain bluebird, he took a week's vacation from work and crossed the state to redrill larger holes in each box. Though not a naturalist by profession, Aylesworth and his efforts prevented these two birds from certain extinction. He counted only five birds in 1974 and 1975. By 1998, the count was 17,567. There are 35,000 memorials to Aylesworth throughout Montana.

She Did, and Let's Just
Leave It at That

Shirley Polykoff, 90, died in New York City on June 4, 1998. She was a star in the advertising world after she created the hugely successful 1956 campaign for Clairol hair dye: "Does she, or doesn't she? . . . Hair color so natural, only her hairdresser knows for sure."

At the time this ad campaign was launched, only 7 percent of American women colored their hair, mostly actresses and "fast" women. Polykoff's alluring ads changed all that. Clairol sales skyrocketed to $100 million the first year of her campaign. Within a decade nearly half of all American women colored their hair. Clairol still accounts for more than half the market, with current annual sales exceeding $1 billion.

A Brooklyn native, Polykoff started her career as a secretary and copywriter. She took pride in her femininity and her blond hair. When she started needing assistance from a hairdresser to keep her hair blond, her future mother-in-law hissed to her son, in Yiddish, "Does she or doesn't she?" Many of her advertising colleagues rejected the Clairol line when they first heard it, because they considered it too suggestive. But when tested on average women, the target market, they didn't find the line suggestive at all. Polykoff soon became executive vice president of Foote, Cone & Belding ad agency, where she wrote other memorable slogans for Clairol, including "Is it true blondes have more fun?" and "If I've only one life to live, let me live it as a blonde."

A pioneering role model for women, Polykoff nevertheless adhered to "being a girl first and an advertising woman second." She held her salary at $25,000 so she would not earn more than her husband, lawyer George Halperin. When he died in 1961, the agency doubled her salary several times. She opened her own agency in 1973.

Photographer to
Emperors

Bruno Zehnder, 52, who made a career out of photographing penguins, died in Antarctica on July 7, 1997. The New York City resident lost his way in a blizzard while trying to return to the Russian base at Mirnyy.

Born in Switzerland in 1945, Zehnder grew up in the small mountain town of Bad Ragaz, near the border of Lichtenstein. He and one of his brothers, Guido, moved to New York City in the 1970s. But Bruno spent most of his time traveling the globe, particularly in Asia, and he spent months at a time in Antarctica as a freelance photographer. His work appeared in dozens of magazines around the world, and he was best known for his photo of a pair of emperor penguins in a tender embrace, a penguin chick between them.

Zehnder would travel from one base to another on

Antarctica, a collection of settlements sponsored by countries such as Russia, Chile, New Zealand, Denmark, and the United States. His primary goal was photographing emperor penguins, the only Antarctic creatures that breed on open sea ice in the continuous darkness, at temperatures as low as minus 70 degrees. In 1984, Zehnder brought his fiancée, Heather May of New York, to the Argentine station at Marambio, Antarctica, where they were married before a group of penguin witnesses. The couple separated three years later.

Zehnder had left Mirnyy station on foot at noon on July 7 and, at 3:40 P.M., he radioed to the station that the weather had deteriorated and he was coming back. No more was heard, and the Russians put out flares to guide Zehnder. The next day, his body was discovered a mile past the base, which he had inadvertently passed by only fifty yards in the dark blizzard. As he requested in his will, Zehnder was buried under the Antarctic ice.

So Shall He Scale the Stars

Dr. Jeffrey A. Willick, 40, was killed by a car in Englewood, New Jersey, on June 18, 2000. Willick was an astrophysicist and assistant professor at Stanford University in California. A native of Bergen County, Willick was a brilliant researcher who wanted everyone to love and understand science as much as he did.

"He said you have to make your work interesting to a wider public, not just to the other five people who are working on what you're working on," said Neta Bahcall, a Princeton astronomer. Willick was a leader in the emerging field of astrophysics, peering through telescopes at galaxies in order to solve great riddles of modern science, such as the weight of the universe. He studied the topography of space intensely, but Willick also loved to teach. A graduate of Harvard and the University of California, Willick taught high school physics before he earned his Ph.D. in physics from Berkeley. He was a superb athlete as well, who loved nothing more than an astronomy conference that took place at a ski resort in the French Alps.

"He was a really normal person," said Pureet Bastra, an astronomy graduate student. "He'd go out and drink a beer with you. He was a good guy."

Willick had traveled to Teaneck, New Jersey, with his two children to visit his father, Martin, for Father's Day. He was sitting with his laptop computer in an Englewood Starbucks coffee shop when a late-model Mustang GT crashed through the window and killed him. Willick was so engrossed in his work, "I don't think he knew what hit him," said a witness, Michelle Radin. The car's driver was charged with driving while intoxicated.

Suffragette Samurai

Mumeo Oku, a lifelong campaigner for women's rights, died in Tokyo on July 7, 1997. She was 101. Oku was also a tireless advocate for consumer's rights and founded Japan's first such advocacy group in 1945, the Housewives' Association, which she led for decades.

"She opened the way for consumers' rights in Japan," said Teiko Kihara, head of Japan's League of Women Voters.

Oku founded the Housewives' Association in the days following World War II, when the government was rationing matches that were so poor in quality that only one in ten would light. The group went on to protest other products, such as clothing that shrank too much, and "canned beef" that turned out to be horse meat or whale meat. Oku led protest marches where women wore aprons over their kimonos and waved rice ladles high in the air.

The daughter of a blacksmith, Oku was born in Fukui prefecture and graduated from Japan Women's University. She became active in the woman's suffrage movement in 1920, and then in the labor movement after she took a job at a spinning company. Oku ran a shelter for poor women and children from 1923 until it was destroyed in 1944 by an American air raid.

When Japanese women won the right to vote and hold office in 1946, Oku won a seat in the upper house of Parliament and served for three six-year terms.

"She always wore a kimono beautifully," said Kihara, "but her mind was tougher than men's. She was very clear in expressing her opinion even in front of men of high status. Very few woman could do that in Japan at that time."

He Shoed Horses

Edward B. C. Keefer, M.D., 84, died April 3, 2000, in Brookville, New York. When Dr. Keefer retired from his practice as a surgeon, he dedicated his retirement to saving thoroughbred horses who were about to be destroyed.

Keefer was born in Biltmore, North Carolina, and went to medical school at McGill University in Montreal. He and his wife moved to Long Island when he went to work as a surgeon at New York Hospital. He also enjoyed windsurfing and polo. The doctor was recruited to help ailing horses at nearby Meadow Brook Fox Hounds in his spare time. When he learned one of the club's horses had cancer of the anal gland, he studied equine anatomy and found it fairly similar to a human's. He removed the tumor and the horse lived another three years.

In 1973, he created an artificial leg for Spanish Riddle, a stablemate of Secretariat. This enabled the horse to live an extra five years in a new career as a stud stallion.

"I had never devised an artificial leg before," said Dr. Keefer. "I went to a guy who built them at the Hospital for Special Surgery, who happened to be an amputee himself. He was a great help to me.

"I also went to see a blacksmith," he added. "I picked everybody's brain. The blacksmith taught me how to weld, and I wound up constructing the artificial leg right here at home. It was basically made of leather with a steel brace. I didn't know if it would work or not."

Spanish Riddle went on to sire several champion horses, including Love Sign, who earned nearly $1 million in the early 1980s.

"This animal . . . deserves most of the credit," said Dr. Keefer. "I saw this horse gallop on an artificial leg. He was awkward, but he could gallop. That was a thrill, a great reward."

Dr. Keefer saved more than a dozen horses, although he was unable to save Ruffian, the most successful filly in racing, whose leg was shattered in 1975. She awoke from anesthesia and cast off the special brace Keefer had made for her.

"She thought she was still galloping in the race," he marveled.

A Man-eater's Man

Perry W. Gilbert, a biologist and shark advocate, died at 87 on October 15, 2000, in Sarasota, Florida. Born in North Branford, Connecticut, Gilbert attended Dartmouth and Cornell universities. He became a professor of comparative anatomy at Cornell in the 1930s, a time when students habitually dissected dead animals, primarly dogfish sharks. Gilbert became fascinated with shark anatomy and soon became the world's foremost authority on sharks. Gilbert's work focused initially on protecting people from sharks. With funding from the Navy, he helped develop chemicals to repel sharks from people in the water. He also helped develop an anesthetic called MS222 that allowed scientists to safely study live sharks.

After Gilbert observed the overfishing of sharks and their degrading environment, his goal shifted to protecting sharks from people. In 1967, Gilbert left Cornell to become director of the Center for Shark Research at Mote Marine Laboratory in Sarasota, then known as Cape Haze. He published several books and articles about every aspect of the shark, including what lessons they might teach to humans about fighting cancer. But Gilbert's greatest challenge was keeping the shark's threat in perspective after the popular *Jaws* movies.

"You're safer in the water than driving to the beach," he would say. "Sharks have survived for 400 million years. The challenge is to find what has allowed them to do this."

Mr. Sviridoff's
Neighborhood

Mitchell Sviridoff, 81, died in New York City on October 21, 2000. Sviridoff was a professor at the New School and an official at the Ford Foundation, but he was best known for spending his life helping the lives of the city's poorest residents. Sviridoff, who was known as Mike, started grassroots organizations to revive neighborhoods such as Bedford-Stuyvesant in Brooklyn. He raised millions of dollars from corporations and foundations to help community development through jobs and low-cost housing.

A native of New Haven, Connecticut, Sviridoff graduated from a vocational school and worked in an aircraft assembly plant. He became involved in the labor movement and eventually became president of the state's AFL-CIO. In the 1960s, he became the head of an antipoverty program in New Haven, which found jobs for

1,500 people in only two years and became a national model during President Johnson's subsequent War on Poverty. In spite of his limited education, Sviridoff became adept at writing grant proposals. Sviridoff moved on to work for the Ford Foundation, where he helped found the Local Initiatives Support Corporation. With his guidance, the group raised $3 billion over two decades, creating 100,000 housing units as well as commercial projects such as East Harlem's first full-size supermarket in 30 years. Sviridoff never had a political agenda, only an abiding desire for an effective approach to getting things done. Those buildings now stand as monuments to his life's work throughout New York City.

Dreamers

King of Hobos
Hops Last Boxcar

Irving Stevens, America's king of the hobos, died on May 4, 1999, at 88. Stevens, elected king of the hobos at the Iowa hobos convention in 1988, was once famous for his homespun advice in newspapers and on television, extolling the virtues of the hobo philosophy.

"Hobos are not tramps," he said. "Tramps get by with begging and perhaps stealing. A hobo is a wandering worker, self-sufficient and prepared to go anywhere for a job."

Great ranches and farms were reliable seasonal work—hence the term *hobo*, which was probably derived from "hoe boy." Some hobos carried their personal hoes from job to job, used the railroads for travel, and got acquainted with one another through a series of nicknames, such as Steamtrain Maury and Choo-Choo Johnson.

Stevens, who was born in Maine, was known as "Fish-bones," because he was very thin.

Stevens wrote two books of hobo anecdotes, *Dear Fishbones* and *Hoboing in the 1930s*. He served in the Air Force during World War II and later settled down in a regular job, married, and had six children. During the 1960s, rail-riding became less popular due to faster diesel engines, vigilant railway companies, and growing job markets. Stevens invented a fly repellent, a foul-smelling concoction called Irving's Fly Dope, which provided him with a regular income in his later years, after he gave up the rails for good.

Countess Swung
a Mean Tray

Felicia Gizycka Magruder died on February 26, 1999, in Laramie, Wyoming. She was 93. Magruder was the former Countess Felicia Gizycka, the only daughter of the Chicago-born newspaper heiress Eleanor Medill Patterson and Count Josef Gizycka, a fortune-hunting scion of a noble Polish family. Patterson was a granddaughter of Joseph Medill, the founder of the *Chicago Tribune*.

Countess Felicia was born in 1905 in Blansko, in what is now the Czech Republic. In 1908, when Felicia was a toddler, her mother ran away from the count after a violent quarrel. The little countess was later reported by newspapers as having been kidnapped in London by the count, who hid her until United States President-elect William Howard Taft intervened in the custody struggle. He wrote to Czar Nicholas II of Russia, in whose realm the Gizycka family estates were located, to "make such order to Count Gizycka as shall seem to Your Majesty equitable."

The Czar commanded that the count return Felicia to her mother, who then bought a ranch in Wyoming. When Felicia was a young woman, a journalist named Drew Pearson came out to court her. But Felicia was not interested, and the teenage countess caught a train to San Diego, where she took an assumed name and supported herself as a waitress.

"I could swing a mean tray," she recalled later. "I always wanted to make my own way in life—it gives one a nice feeling."

Undeterred, Pearson caught up with her. He was not yet the mighty syndicated newspaper columnist he would become, but he is said to have made her a practical offer: "Look, you're only 18. Marry me now and in three years, if you don't love me, you can leave and start your life all over again." Their marriage began in 1925, produced a daughter, Ellen, and after three years, Mrs. Pearson sought her divorce. She moved to New York and elsewhere, wrote articles for American magazines and newspapers, in addition to novels and short stories. In her 1939 novel *Flower of Smoke*, her Austrian-American heroine says, "Make your own peace, no matter what."

Her 1934 marriage to an Englishman, Dudley de Lavigne, ended in divorce. Her 1958 marriage to John Kennedy Magruder, a landscape architect and a director of the Alcoholics Anonymous Men's Home in Alexandria, Virginia, also ended in divorce.

Poker Champ
Folds Last Hand

Stuey Ungar, the tenth grade dropout who first won the World Series of Poker when he was 23 years old, died on November 21, 1998, at age 45.

Ungar was New York's greatest card player ever, with a killer instinct and a disregard for money that made him unbeatable, but also a lifelong taste for fast living that forced his last hand.

He was born and raised in the East Village of Manhattan, a gambler's paradise in the days before lotteries and off-track betting. Stuey was always a whiz with numbers and started playing cards with busboys during his summer vacations in the Catskills. When his father died, he dropped out of high school and started playing poker. He also seemed to stop growing that year. At five feet five inches tall, he never weighed more than 100 pounds, but he was a bundle of hyperactive energy who disarmed other players.

"When he was completely focused, Stuey could see things that other people didn't," said one gambler. "He was a genius."

By the time he was 17, Stuey hung out at clubs, fraternizing with gangsters and gamblers, playing poker in dark rooms in every neighborhood of Manhattan. At 20, he moved in with Madeline Wheeler, a waitress from Queens. When he ran up a $60,000 debt to a loan shark, he absconded to Las Vegas to earn it back. This childlike New Yorker with the thuggish patter was 22 years old, and quickly won more than $1 million in Vegas. Madeline moved west, the two were married and soon had a daughter.

Ungar had never played no-limit hold-em when he signed up for the World Series of Poker (entry fee: $10,000). He won the $365,000 prize in 1980 and was soon dubbed "Mr. Las Vegas." He appeared on the *Merv Griffin Show* and started dressing in Versace shirts to set off his pageboy hairstyle. In 1981, Ungar won the World Series again, gambling away his winnings and loving every minute of Las Vegas.

"We'd lose track of how high the stakes were," said Mickey Appleman, a fellow gambler. "Action was an end to itself."

Ungar gave large celebrations when he won big. Then he started betting on golf, which was not a strong sport for him. He craved big action. He bet on sports games, losing $1 million on one football game. Losing depressed him, and he started bingeing on cocaine. His marriage ended in 1989, and he lost his house. By 1990, people stopped seeing him around the casinos.

In 1997, Las Vegas had evolved into a family destination resort, but Stuey Ungar reappeared at the World Series of Poker, where he won $1 million. He took his winnings to bet on sports games and to party, running through his prize in just four months. He died of natural causes at the Oasis Motel in Las Vegas, right after he'd registered to play in a December tournament at the Taj Mahal in Atlantic City.

Kissing Communist

Galina Breshneva, the 68-year-old daughter of former Soviet leader Leonid Breshnev, died in
Moscow in July 1998. A notorious beauty, Galina was
married four times, always to men far younger than
herself. Much to her father's chagrin, two of her husbands were circus performers, for whom she had a
particular predilection. Her sister Svetlana left for a
modest life in the West as a young woman, but Galina
lived a wild life of conspicuous extravagance in the Soviet Union. And the Russian people did not begrudge
Breshneva her fancy cars and jewels. Long after her father had died and many of her friends were jailed for
corruption, Galina lived on with a full pension in a
Moscow apartment and her dacha in the country. She
was survived by her 29-year-old husband.

Fantasia Hippo's
Final Bow

Tatiana Riabouchinska, 83, died in Los Angeles on August 24, 2000. One of the famed "baby ballerinas" of the Ballet Russe de Monte Carlo in the 1930s, Riabouchinska's family had escaped house arrest in Moscow during the Russian Revolution. Her father had been a banker for the czar, but the family's servants helped them escape to France. When George Balanchine spotted her dancing at age 15 in Paris, he signed her to the Ballet Russe, where she created dance roles in *Jeux d'Enfants*, *Les Presages*, *La Concurrence*, and *Graduation Ball*. She danced into the early 1950s, performing works by George Balanchine, Leonide Massine, and David Lichine, whom she married in 1943. She was celebrated for the joy and warmth of her style, her high leaps and exquisite arms.

In 1940, illustrators working for the Walt Disney

Company sketched Riabouchinska during rehearsals in Los Angeles. She was then transformed into the unforgettable hippopotamus ballerina in the celebrated animated film *Fantasia*. Her husband was the model for the film's alligator. The couple moved to Los Angeles in 1950, where Lichine died in 1972. Riabouchinska continued to teach ballet until her death.

Last of the
Red Sox Lovers

Elizabeth Dooley, 87, died in Boston on June 19, 2000. She saw more than 4,000 consecutive Red Sox games in more than 55 seasons at Fenway Park. Only hours after her death, the Red Sox suffered their most humiliating defeat ever: 22–1 to the New York Yankees.

Dooley was raised in Boston and taught there in the public school system for thirty-nine years. Her father, John Stephen Dooley, helped Boston support the new team in the late nineteenth century. Family lore has it that he attended every opening game of the Red Sox from 1894 until his death in 1970 at age 97.

His daughter began attending Fenway games during World War II, a passion that grew from her aversion to bridge, the more fashionable ladies' pastime of the era. She quickly became a fixture at Fenway, bringing Oreos and Starburst candies to players and telephoning Ted Williams every year on his birthday. She never married and never missed a home game for more than fifty years.

"I have always considered myself a friend of not only the Red Sox but the whole game," Dooley said once. "Being a friend means being there from the 'Star-Spangled Banner' to the final out."

She was, in the words of Ted Williams, "the greatest Red Sox fan there'll ever be." Before the June 19 Red Sox–Yankees game, fans stood to honor Dooley with a moment of silence before the national anthem.

2030:
A Human Race Oddity

FM-2030, the 69-year-old futurist, author, and Miami resident, died in New York City on July 8, 2000. He was "launched," as he liked to say, in 1930 as F. M. Esfandiary, the son of an Iranian diplomat in Belgium, but changed his name to FM-2030 in the mid 1970s. He lived in seventeen countries during his first eleven years and preferred to think of himself as a global citizen in a universe where there should be no borders. He never revealed what the FM stood for ("Future Man?"), but the significance of 2030 may have been for the one hundredth year of his birth.

A sunny optimist with the futuristic vision that all people will eventually be completely made of synthetic parts, he was a handsome and dashing man who spoke fluent Arabic, French, Hebrew, and English. He competed for Iran in the 1948 Olympics, in both basketball and wrestling. He wrote extensively about an imaginary future, where three-dimensional objects could be reproduced by "copying machines," the sun would be our primary (and free) energy source, and humans would be immortal. In the spirit of Jules Verne, FM-2030 predicted certain technologies long before they came to be, such as human fertilization outside the body, teleconferencing, and teleshopping.

"I am a twenty-first-century person who was accidentally born into the twentieth," FM-2030 once said. "I have a deep nostalgia for the future."

FM-2030 taught at the New School for Social Research in New York City and UCLA, and was a consultant for Lockheed, JC Penney, and Florida International University. He wrote several novels, including *Identity Card* in 1966, which novelist Anne Tyler praised during the 1979 Iranian revolution as "the perfect way to find out why so many fists are raised in Iran today." FM-2030 is survived by four sisters and one brother. His body is frozen in liquid nitrogen in Scottsdale, Arizona.

Fred and Ginger
of the Fairway

Kay Farrell, a stylish golfer who was married to the 1928 U.S. Open golf champion Johnny Farrell, died on July 12, 1997, in Village of Golf, Florida. She was 86.

The couple met in 1930, when Farrell intentionally hit a shot that rolled to her feet at Innis Arden Golf Club in Old Greenwich, Connecticut. She was a teenager selling programs during a golf exhibition. The renowned Farrell was a champion golfer who had recently beat Bobby Jones in a thrilling playoff by a single shot. She soon broke up with her beau at the time, future New York City mayor Robert F. Wagner Jr., and Farrell broke up with his girlfriend, the actress Fay Wray. Kay and Johnny were married in 1931, and they promptly produced a number of instructional "talking pictures," in which Farrell taught his bride how to properly swing a club. They played golf with celebrities, such as Douglas Fairbanks

Jr. and Babe Ruth. When Farrell became golf pro at Baltusrol Golf Club in Springfield, New Jersey, Kay helped the women's team win the 1948 state championship. The couple were noted for their elegant attire and splendid dancing.

While Johnny became a golf instructor to such students as the Duke of Windsor and Richard Nixon, Kay had five children and entertained constantly. Their children became superb golfers in their own right, and in 1967 the Metropolitan Golf Writers Association named the Farrells the golf family of the year. Johnny died in 1988 at age 87.

King of the Conch Republic

Mel Fisher died at age 76 on December 19, 1998, in Key West, after spending years diving for sunken treasure. Many people called him a no-good scavenger, but when he was 62 he hit paydirt. He uncovered what he called a "lobster condo" 41 miles off Key West, which turned out to be stacks of silver bars. Nearby were a fortune in gold, emeralds, diamonds, and pearls lost on a seventeenth-century Spanish ship.

Fisher was born in Hobart, Indiana, and had an early interest in diving. As a child, he recalled, he tried to make his own breathing apparatus with a five-gallon paint can and a bicycle pump. He moved with his parents in 1950 to work on a chicken ranch in California, where he opened a small dive shop on the property, then a retail store in Redondo Beach: Mel's Aqua Shop.

By 1960, Fisher owned a diving boat known as the

Golden Doubloon, a converted Navy towing vessel. He scoured the California coast, then moved on to the Caribbean, where there were many more shipwrecks. He met a Floridian named Kip Wagner, also a treasure hunter, and made the move to work full-time with Wagner. In 1968, he started a search for the *Nuestra Senora de Atocha* and the *Santa Margarita,* both from an ill-fated Spanish fleet lost in 1622. Three years later, he found pieces of the *Atocha,* and ten years after that, he found the *Santa Margarita*—but still no massive treasures. Finally, in 1985, two of his crew members found the "lobster condo" under 55 feet of water, and with it the mother lode of jewels valued at $400 million. Naturally, the state of Florida and the U.S. government arrived to stake part of the claim, which caused protracted legal battles. Fisher was crowned "King of the Conch Republic" in Key West, and he liked to wear gold chains from the recovered treasure.

Madcap Maestro

L ouis "Moondog" Hardin died at age 83 on September 8, 1999, in Munster, Germany. He was well known in New York City as the mysterious "Viking of Sixth Avenue," a street person who stood sentry at 54th Street and the Avenue of the Americas (Sixth Avenue) for more than thirty years, beginning in the late 1940s.

Born in Kansas in 1916, Hardin was blinded at age 16 by an exploding dynamite blasting cap. While attending the Iowa School for the Blind, he became obsessed with becoming a musical composer. He arrived in New York City in 1943 and camped outside the stage entrance to Carnegie Hall until he met Artur Rodzinksi, conductor of the New York Philharmonic. Mr. Rodzinski was taken with the young man and promised to conduct Hardin's music, if he ever composed some. But he couldn't write his music like sighted people, and he was unable to afford assistance in writing out a score. So Hardin changed his name to Moondog and earned a living as a street musician, performing percussion improvisations. Hardin was usually dressed in a flowing cape and a Viking helmet, with homemade sandals and a large spear at his side. He said this outfit reflected his "Nordic philosophy."

In the mid 1950s, long after Rodzinksi had left the Philharmonic, Hardin somehow succeeded in recording the "Moondog Symphony," which was frequently played on the radio by pioneering rock and roll disc jockey Alan Freed. In the 1960s, Hardin obtained access to an orchestra and recorded an album for CBS called *Moondog*. But his adherence to Viking dress ultimately led to his eviction from Philharmonic rehearsals.

He was celebrated by the beat poets for his verbal broadsides against government control and organized religion, wrote music for radio commercials, and found success when Janis Joplin recorded his song, "All Is Loneliness," and another composition was used in the 1972 film, *Drive, He Said*, starring Jack Nicholson.

When he was invited to West Germany in 1974 to perform his music, he left his post on Sixth Avenue to perform on the streets of Europe. He was taken in by a German family who helped him transcribe his compositions from Braille, and he produced five albums during his later years. He regularly performed his compositions with chamber and symphony orchestras in Germany as well as in Paris and Stockholm.